In the Deep, Dark Ocean

Written by John Suzuki
Illustrated by Dion Hamill

Ballena was a blue whale.
In winter, she lived in the warm water
off the coast of South America.

Now, it was the first week of summer.
She was going to swim south
to the cool waters of Antarctica
to eat tiny sea creatures called krill.

Ballena was just about ready to go.

First, Ballena had to join the other whales.
Ballena was looking forward to swimming with her friends.

The whales were gathering together.
Ballena joined them, looking for her friends.
Only the young whales like Ballena were here now.
The adult whales, like Ballena's mother, were already gone.

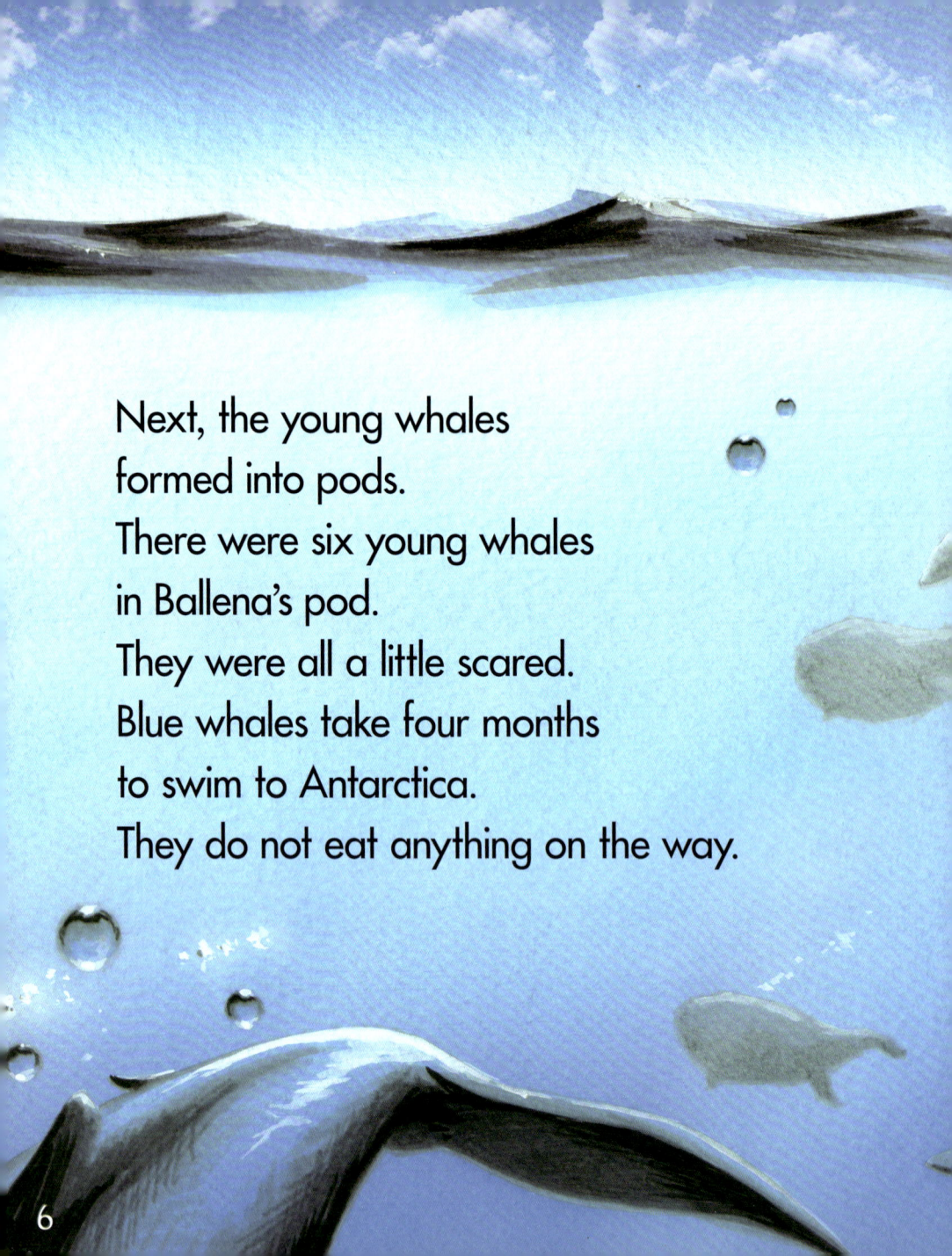

Next, the young whales
formed into pods.
There were six young whales
in Ballena's pod.
They were all a little scared.
Blue whales take four months
to swim to Antarctica.
They do not eat anything on the way.

Then, the pod began its journey.
It was the second week of summer.
There were big birds called albatrosses
flying in the sky.

"They don't look very big to me,"
Ballena told the whale next to her.

Ballena was trying to act tough.
In fact, she was scared.
This was her first time swimming
out into the deep, dark ocean
without her mother.

Soon after that, the pod left the coast
of South America.
The young whales swam out
into the deep, dark ocean.
Ballena's heart beat fast.
She wasn't scared
when her mother was with her.
Now, though…
She wasn't ready
to dive deep by herself.

After a week, the other young whales
dived deep.
Ballena stayed at the surface.

While the other whales were gone,
Ballena talked to an albatross.
The albatross was going to Antarctica, too.

"I went to Antarctica once
when I was young," said the albatross.
"I want to see it again."

Two months later, there was a storm.
The sky went dark and the surface
of the ocean grew rough.
Ballena tried to swim
through the raging, swirling water.

Soon, the albatross saw
that Ballena was in trouble.

"Dive below the water!"
shouted the albatross.

"No, I can't!" cried Ballena.

"You must, Ballena!" screamed the albatross.
"It's the only way
you will make it through the storm!"

The rest of the pod had already dived.
At last, Ballena took a deep breath
and dived down under the water.

Deep down, the ocean water was dark.
There were strange fish.
Ballena heard strange noises.
She could hear the pod, too.
The blue whales were talking to one another.
Ballena started to feel less scared.
Maybe it wasn't so bad after all.

The next day, when the storm was over,
the pod swam on.
The ocean was getting colder now.
After such a long swim,
the young blue whales were very hungry.
There would be a lot of krill to eat
when they reached their goal.

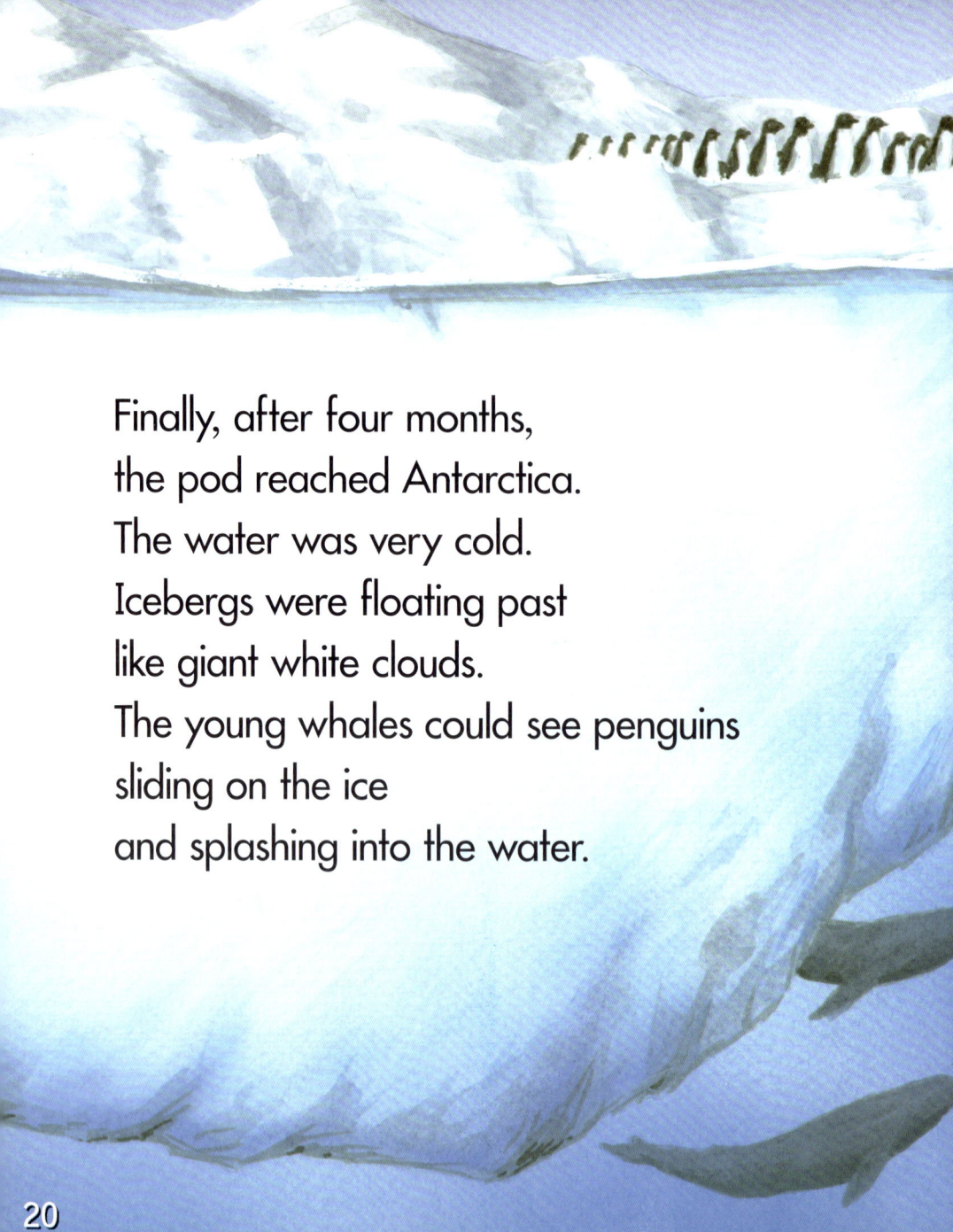

Finally, after four months,
the pod reached Antarctica.
The water was very cold.
Icebergs were floating past
like giant white clouds.
The young whales could see penguins
sliding on the ice
and splashing into the water.

One week later, Ballena heard
a voice that she knew well.
In the distance,
she could see her mother
gliding across the top of the water.

"Hello, mother!" called out Ballena.
"We have made it all the way by ourselves."

"Well done, Ballena!
I am so proud of you,"
said her mother.